Ruby & Rufus

Olivier Dunrea

Houghton Mifflin Harcourt

Boston New York

hmhco.com

The text of this book was set in Shannon.
The illustrations in this book were done in pen and ink and gouache
on 140-pound d'Arches coldpress watercolor paper.

Library of Congress Cataloging-in-Publication Data is on file.

ISBN: 978-0-547-86760-1

Manufactured in China
SCP 10 9 8 7 6 5 4 3 2 1
4500743117

For our beloved Molly and Gabe
who love the water!

This is Ruby.

This is Rufus.

Ruby loves to swan dive into the pond.

Rufus loves to back dive into the pond.

Ruby and Rufus love the water.

They swim on the pond all day.

They swim in the rain.

They swim when it's windy.

Ruby stands on her head underwater.

Rufus chases fish across the water.

Ruby and Rufus swim on the pond.

Every day.

One cold winter morning, Ruby and
Rufus scamper to the pond.

The water is frozen!

Ruby taps the ice with her bill.

Rufus taps the ice with his foot.

"Ice!" honks Ruby.

"Ice?" honks Rufus.

Ruby slides across
the ice on her feet.

Rufus slides across
the ice on his chin.

They streak across the ice!

Ruby and Rufus love the frozen pond!

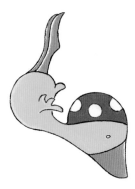

This is Ruby.
She loves to dive.

This is Rufus.
He loves to swim.

This is Ruby.
She loves to slide.

This is Rufus.
He loves to glide.

Ruby and Rufus love the pond
all year round.